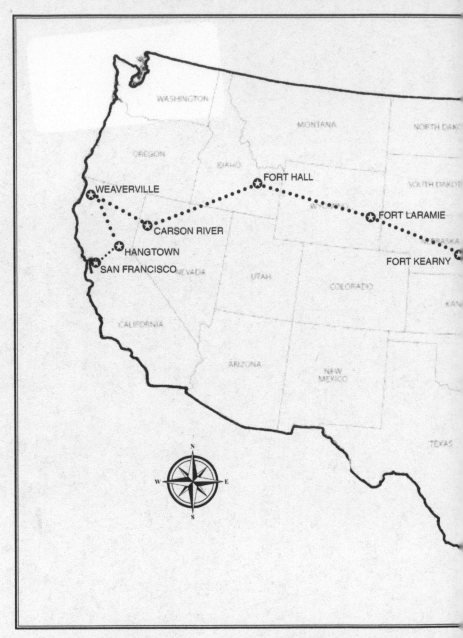

Horseback, stagecoach, train, canal boat, paddle-wheel steamboat, covered wagon and by foot, this is the route Eugene Chase took in 1849 from Derby Line, Vermont (top right) to the gold fields of California (far left) in Weaverville and Hangtown. The route was over 3000 miles and took five months from

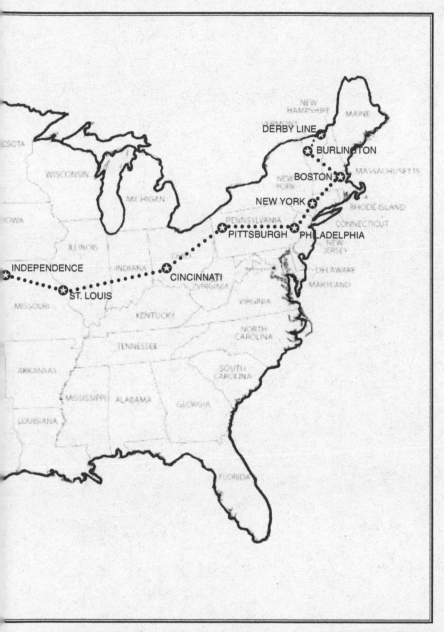

beginning to end. Eugene estimated that he walked some 1000 miles on foot. Between 1835 and 1855 nearly 10,000 deaths occurred along the trail. Food, water, and firewood were scarce. The journey was a severe test of strength and endurance. Eugene chose to make the trip home via sailing ship, leaving from San Francisco.

Here to There and Back Again

Here to There and Back Again

Gail Wilson Kenna

To Patty
my pleasure to
have you in classes.

Gail

With illustrations by
Chris Edwards

Crosshill Creek Publications

Printed in the United States of America

Crosshill Creek Publications
P. O. Box 216, Wicomico Church, VA 22579

This book was designed and produced by Hearth & Garden Productions

A. Cort Sinnes, Design

Library of Congress Cataloging-in-Publication Data

Kenna, Gail Wilson *Here to There and Back Again*

written by Gail Wilson Kenna

ISBN 978-1-7341602-2-2

Front cover: Adapted from *Crossing the Prairie* by Jules Tavernier, c. 1850

"We are encamped on a large prairie; the scenery is very grand; we can see miles off. I wish you were here to see it with me."

Eugene B. Chase, in a letter to his sister, 1849

In memory of

Eugene B. Chase
and
Eugene Chase McLaren

Table of Contents

Prologue

In the summer of 1979, I visited my maternal grandmother in our family's old mountain cabin. Built in the 1920s, the cabin borders the Sequoia National Forest of California. Since childhood in the 1950s I'd loved Poso Park. I chased butterflies in the meadows, fished for trout in the creek, ran through the dark forest without fear. At home in Fullerton, close to Los Angeles, there were nuclear war worries. Yet under my school desk during hydrogen bomb drills, I knew there was a safe place in the world—the cabin and creek in Poso Park.

Over two decades later, I'd gone to the mountains to say good-bye to my grandmother. I wanted my young daughters to see her before we left California. My husband had received Air Force orders. We were moving to Montgomery, Alabama. A native of California, I did not want to move anywhere else. And the thought of leaving the Napa Valley was distressing. I was an English teacher at Vintage High. I had many wonderful friends. I especially did not want to leave our unique stone house on Soda Canyon Creek.

My grandmother sensed my unhappiness. One evening after the children went to bed, she and I sat before the cabin's rock fireplace. Each one of the rocks had come from Poso Creek. Nights are chilly in the mountains. We built a small fire and sat before it, going through a big box of albums and memorabilia. My deceased grandfather, Eugene McLaren, treasured everything old. On the back of photographs, he had identified people and places. I could have sat there all night looking through the albums. Yet Grandmother was yawning. I could see she was tired. A spunky woman at eighty-four, she did need her sleep. She began repacking the box, then stopped.

"I don't think you've ever read these old letters."

She handed me a black and maroon ledger. It was the kind that Grandfather used for accounts. A Scottish storekeeper and postmaster, he had called himself.

"What is this?" I asked.

"Your great-great grandfather's Gold Rush letters."

She explained that someone in Derby Line, Vermont, had copied the letters into the ledger.

"Look inside at the inscription," she said. "The book was given to your grandfather Eugene. Did you know he always signed his name, Eugene Chase McLaren in honor of his great-great grandfather, Eugene B. Chase."

I didn't know any of it. Grandfather had died

when I was twelve. I had felt close to him and relished his humorous stories. Yet I knew little about his life. I said good-night and went to the front bedroom. There I opened two windows to hear the creek gurgling over its bed of rocks, just yards from the cabin. I crawled in the old double bed with its thick comforter. I turned on a small lamp on the nightstand. A beam of light fell directly on the book. I began with the first letter and did not stop until I had read the last one.

My great-great grandfather's voice spoke to me. I heard him say, "It's hard to leave one place for another. It's hard to be alone and uncertain. It's hard to keep your feet moving when they beg to stop. But don't quit. Above all else, do not give up."

When I left Poso Park that summer, I carried Eugene B. Chase's book of letters with me. I knew that one day I would tell his story in my own words.

Here is that story.

Gail Wilson Kenna

Chapter I

Furrows in the Field

The day was hot for early fall. Eugene had been putting in fence posts all morning and felt tired. He stopped digging and looked at the sky. Clouds in the distance told him a summer storm was coming. The rain would make the air humid. In the wet, warm air it would be harder to work. Eugene pulled his shirt away from his chest. He leaned on his shovel and looked across the fields. Furrows. Rows of them. Each laid out like all the others.

Eugene heard his name. He thought it was his father telling him to get back to work. He turned. Near the south field, he saw Leal atop his mare. He was riding bareback, wore no shirt, and waved at Eugene. Leal was headed for the river to swim until the hot afternoon passed. Eugene called, "I can't go."

"Be by later," Leal shouted as he rode away. Eugene stared at the sky again. When he was tired he often looked upward. Was the sky in the West like the sky in the East, he wondered?

He heard his name again.

"Eugene."

This time it *was* his father. As always, the furrows called Eugene back to earth.

That evening as Eugene's family sat down to supper, Leal knocked on the door.

"Will you have supper with us, Leal?" Eugene's mother asked.

"Nah," he said. "Just need to talk to Eugene."

Eugene looked at his father. "Five minutes, Father." He rose from the table and stepped outside the house.

Leal took a piece of paper from his pocket. "My aunt brought some papers from Boston. Look what I found in one."

Eugene read the newspaper advertisement Leal handed him. "The Pioneer Line to California? What's this about?"

"They've found gold out there. A big strike. I'm going to send for these pamphlets."

Eugene gave little thought to what Leal told him that night. Derby Line, Vermont, was thousands of miles from California. Then Eugene began to hear rumors in town. One Saturday he and his father went into Derby Line for supplies. Everywhere Eugene heard talk about gold in California. He questioned the storekeeper.

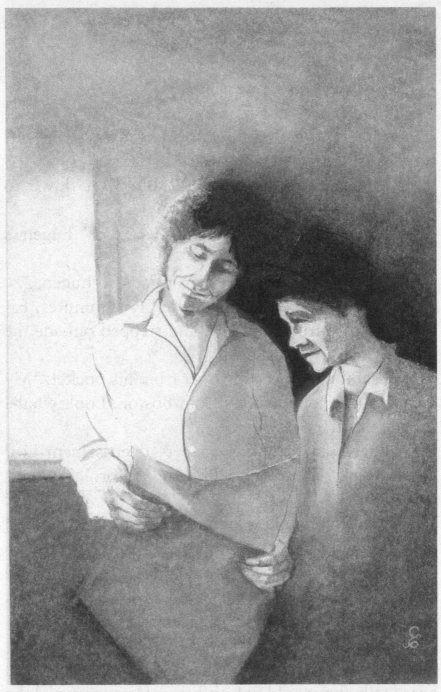

Eugene and Leal read the front page newspaper story about the discovery of gold in California.

"Do you think these rumors are true?"

"Can't say for certain. I read a man mined twenty thousand in six days."

Eugene's father laughed. "Fool's gold. That's what they're mining."

"What if it isn't a rumor, Father?"

"There will be plenty of fools heading to California whether it is rumor or not."

Eugene's father always said the only thing worse than a fool was the devil. For that reason, Eugene didn't mention California again. Yet while he worked in the fields he thought about the West.

In early November, Leal gave Eugene a pamphlet from the Pioneer Line. Eugene took it home. After everyone had gone to bed, he studied the detailed brochure. The next day he saw Leal.

"This Pioneer Line sounds good. Too bad I don't have that kind of money."

"Your Uncle does."

Eugene didn't answer Leal. He couldn't ask to borrow money from Uncle Lucien based on rumors.

Then a day in December changed Eugene's mind. He had gone into Derby Line and seen a newspaper with the boldest headline he remembered. He couldn't wait to show the paper to his father.

He didn't rush into the house with the news. He waited while his sister and mother cleared the table from supper. Then he spread the newspaper in front of his father.

"Is President Polk about to tell rumors to the Congress, Father?"

"What is it, Eugene?" His three brothers leaned closer.

"President Polk has announced the Gold Rush."

Eugene's father read the paper slowly. He handed it back to Eugene and said nothing.

That night Eugene waited downstairs until everyone had gone to bed. He sat at his father's desk and wrote a letter.

December 22, 1848

Dear Uncle Lucien,
It is my desire to go to California. If you
will lend me the money, I promise to
repay all that I borrow. I must be in St.
Louis no later than late April.

Your nephew,
Eugene

As Eugene sealed the letter, he thought about the months ahead. In a month, he would be nineteen years old. In three months, he would leave home.

Eugene looked out the window into the winter night. The West was out there, though it felt far away.

Chapter II

Letter in Town

Eugene leaned against the fireplace and sipped his morning tea. From the bedroom his mother spoke to him. Then she walked into the kitchen and repeated her question.

"We're almost out of sugar. Is that on the list?"

"Yes Mother."

"You won't forget?"

"No, I won't forget."

Mrs. Chase hurried from the room. Eugene leaned against the fireplace and watched his sister at work in the kitchen. Beneath Hortense's hands was a mound of dough. He walked over to the table.

"How do you make this bread?"

His sister stopped kneading the dough. "Is my brother going to become a baker?"

Eugene brushed some flour from her chin. "Would you like to ride to town with me this morning?"

"Oh, I would like that, Eugene." She wiped her hands on her apron. "You can knead this while I get ready. Mind the dough doesn't stick to your callouses."

"No more than it does to yours," he teased.

Within the hour, they left for town. Neither spoke for the first few miles. Hortense closed her eyes and turned her face to the sun.

"It feels almost like spring today, doesn't it?"

Eugene nodded. He hadn't noticed the day. Winter storms had kept him from town. He hadn't been to Derby Line in two weeks. Would there be a letter today?

When they reached town, Eugene handed Hortense the list of dry goods. "I'll get the mail while you start on this."

On Saturday mornings a line formed at the post office window. When his turn came, Eugene was handed a letter postmarked New York City. He stepped quickly away from the window and opened it.

January 20, 1849

Dear Eugene,
I say, go West young man. I will gladly offer my help. I suggest you come to New York City as soon as possible. My temporary residence is the Astor House.

Ask for me there. I am most curious what my brother and his wife think of their elder son's adventure and of you writing to me. This story and others must wait until we see one another. It has been far too long.

Uncle Lucien

Eugene folded the letter and put it in his pocket. Hortense had filled their order. After a stop at the feed store, they started home. As they crossed the covered bridge outside Derby Line, Eugene handed his sister the letter.

"I never read this," she said, glancing away.

"What do you mean?"

"If you first share your plans with me, Mother and Father will not forgive me."

"It is I they won't forgive. Not you."

"No, Eugene. You are wrong. Mother will refuse to talk to you and take to her bed. In time, she will forgive you. So will Father. You're the eldest son."

"Is that all you have to say?" Eugene looked at his sister and waited.

"No," she said. "Were I a young man, California is where I would go. I'm going to ask a favor, brother. Promise to keep a diary. So one day, I will know what you saw and did."

Eugene looked over at Hortense and said, "I

promise."

"There's something else, Eugene. Don't address letters to Father and Mother. Address your letters to me. I will read them aloud to the family. Mother and Father will only pretend not to listen."

Eugene reached over and took his sister's hand. "I'm not going away forever. You know that, don't you?"

"I know, and I understand why you're going. That's why I say to keep a diary. Not only for me. For your children one day."

"I wish you were going, Hortense."

"To bake your bread, no doubt."

Eugene laughed. "That's possibly true." Just then, the Chase farm came into view.

"Will you be going by yourself?" Hortense asked.

"Leal wants to join me."

Hortense looked over at Eugene, then looked away. "You know how I feel about Leal."

Chapter III

The Weight of Home

Eugene stood close to the fireplace and warmed his hands. The morning had the feel of late winter, not early spring. His mother sat near the fire, darning socks. Eugene watched the fire for several minutes before he spoke.

"I'm leaving for California in a few days."

Eugene's mother continued darning and did not look up.

"I'll be gone no more than two years. Father will get along fine."

Eugene's mother raised her head and pointed the needle at him. "That's more than I can say for you, Eugene Chase. You'll likely get an Indian arrow in your heart. Or drown in a crossing. Or turn to drink and gambling."

"Mother," he said slowly. "I'll not drink. And I'll not gamble."

25

"You say that standing here. What do you know of death or evil? Death's face is ugly, Eugene."

He looked away from his mother and walked over to the kitchen window. He watched blackbirds swoop past. Turning from the window he said, "Mother, I must go West."

She set her darning basket beside the rocker. She walked slowly to the bedroom and lay on the bed, her face to the wall.

Eugene waited by the window until he heard Hortense on the stairs. She pointed to the door. Once outside, she led Eugene away from the house.

"She didn't close the door, did she? When Mother is hurt she takes to her bed. But she leaves the door open."

"I don't mean to hurt Mother."

"I know that. Don't you understand? She will suffer whether you go or stay."

Hortense put her arms around Eugene and held him. "I've something for you." She took a small book from her apron pocket. "It's new. You haven't forgotten your promise, have you?"

Eugene leafed the diary's empty pages. "No," he said. "I have not forgotten. I will keep a diary. Now I must tell Father."

"Father will be easy," she said. "He'll declare you're a fool. That will be the end of it."

Eugene walked to the south field. His three brothers were nearby, uprooting a diseased oak.

"We thought you'd mistaken today for Sunday," his father called.

"I stayed to talk to Mother."

His father leaned on his hoe. "About what, may I ask?"

"About going to California."

"I expected as much. You have money I don't know about?"

"Enough to get to New York. Uncle Lucien has offered to loan me the money I need."

"You expect me to drive you to the stagecoach? Lose a morning's work?"

Eugene looked at his father's weary face. He suspected his father had been waiting a long time for this news.

"Leal will take me."

"Leal going with you?"

"He talks of joining me."

"You're a bigger fool than I thought, Eugene."

"Hortense said you'd say that."

"Hortense in on this, too?"

"No," Eugene quickly replied. "She overheard me talking to Mother." Eugene looked past his father's face and watched Enoch, George, and Arthur fell the oak.

"Father, I want nothing more than to farm. But often I look at the sky and wonder how far it reaches."

"Say no more, Eugene. I won't forbid your jour-

Eugene told his father about his intention to go West to the gold fields of California.

ney. So be it."

They stood in silence. Then Eugene turned and walked across the fields to the barn. There he saddled his mare. He rode across the north field. At the edge of the field was the forest to the Hill farm.

The winter snow had broken branches along the path. Eugene stopped to clear them away. The forest had always been a part of Eugene's life. Trees comforted. Trees protected. Hard as Eugene tried, he could not imagine a land like the Plains without trees.

Eugene rode out of the forest and saw Leal's father. "Good morning, Mr. Hill."

"Morning, Eugene! Leal's in the house."

Eugene found Leal upstairs.

"I need a ride to the stagecoach next week," he said.

Leal turned when he heard Eugene's voice.

"He said yes? Your uncle said yes?"

Eugene nodded.

"Give you a ride? What do you mean? I'm going, too."

"Not to New York. I haven't seen my uncle in eight years."

"We're going together. That's what we planned."

"I'll be in St. Louis by the end of April. If you're serious, join me. Leave here in the next week. We'll be on the river the same time."

"If I'm serious?" Leal walked to his desk and

lifted a stack of pamphlets. "All winter I've thought of nothing but going West."

"I know that."

Leal walked back to where Eugene stood. "Did you tell your father?"

"Yes. Father said I'm a fool."

"Wait till we find a nugget the size of your father's fist."

"We've got to get to California first," Eugene laughed.

"I can already see the gold, Eugene. Right before my eyes."

The train tracks to Burlington, to Boston, and to New York City were all Eugene could see. Yet in Leal's mind, they had reached journey's end.

Chapter IV

Company of the Devil

Spitting and hissing, the train pushed its belly slowly down the tracks. Soot flew through the window into Eugene's face. He closed the window. He sat back in the seat. The train's crude noises and smells did not seem to bother other passengers. They ate candy, read newspapers, chewed tobacco. Eugene had never seen so many strange faces.

The hours passed. The miles stretched before him. His legs began to ache. He walked up and down the aisle. The train jerked along, threw him against the seats. He sat down, felt numb and alone. Eugene thought about what was ahead. There would be a long wait in Boston. Then another train to New York. Eugene leaned back in his seat. He listened to the train grind its way down the tracks. He closed his eyes. The sound grew smoother. He slept.

It took two days to reach New York City. Eugene heard the conductor's call. Stretching his legs, he lifted his satchel and left the train. He wanted to find Uncle Lucien's residence hotel before dark. Once outside the station, he stood without moving. Carriages stopped and sped away. People hurried past. Everyone seemed to have a place to go. Eugene watched a man in fine clothes hurry toward a waiting carriage.

"Sir," Eugene called out. "Could you tell me where the Astor House might be?"

The man tipped his hat and smiled. "The Astor House? Come along, I'm going that way."

The gentleman's driver took Eugene's satchel. He opened the door and Eugene stepped inside. "The Astor is a fine hotel," the man said. Beside this elegant gentleman, Eugene felt unkempt.

"My uncle lives at the Astor temporarily," Eugene remarked.

The gentleman's two bay horses arched their necks and trotted down the street. Eugene answered the questions he was asked. He told the man of his journey West. Yet his eyes sought the streets. So many people bustling everywhere. He looked up, past large buildings to the naked sky.

The carriage stopped. "The Astor House, young man."

"May I pay you something, sir?"

The gentleman smiled. "Perhaps when you find your gold. Not today."

Eugene stood on the street and watched the

carriage move away. He faced the Astor House and counted its five stories. A carriage stopped behind him. Three gentlemen got out. They started up the steps of the hotel. Eugene followed them.

Once inside the lobby, the men approached a long, gleaming desk. Eugene waited until the men had spoken to the clerk. After they left, he approached the desk. The busy clerk spoke without raising his head. "May I help you?"

"My Uncle Lucien, please."

The clerk looked up and smiled. "Excuse me?"

Feeling embarassed, Eugene cleared his throat and lowered his voice. "Lucien Chase, please. Is he in?"

"Always by six, sir. If you'll leave your name, I'll tell Mr. Chase you're here."

Eugene picked up his satchel. "Eugene Chase," he replied. He paused a moment and studied the lobby. He wanted to watch people enter the hotel. Armchairs beneath a window faced the entrance. He went over and sat in one. He hadn't seen his uncle in almost eight years. He wondered if Uncle Lucien would recognize him.

Eugene watched as people entered and left the hotel. He noticed what everyone wore. Hortense would want to know about that, though there were few women. An hour passed, then Eugene saw a dapper man enter the hotel. Eugene recognized the brisk walk of a man approaching the desk. The clerk pointed in Eugene's direction. The man whirled and opened his arms.

Uncle Lucien believed in Eugene's dream and loaned him the money to travel to California and mine for gold.

Eugene wanted to shout Uncle Lucien's name. He wanted to run across the lobby. To whoop and laugh and yell. To be the boy his uncle remembered. Seeing his uncle erased the long miles behind him.

Uncle Lucien held Eugene at arm's length. "Damn. I believe you're taller than your father."

"And you're shorter than I remember, Uncle Lucien." For the first time since leaving Boston, Eugene laughed.

"You must be hungry," his uncle said.

At last Eugene felt the hunger in his stomach.

"Very hungry."

"Come along," he said, lifting Eugene's satchel. "We ought to celebrate your arrival in New York with champagne. But your mother would never forgive you or me."

"She'd say I dined with the devil," Eugene laughed.

"Ah, the evil drink. It's good I left Derby Line. Tonight we will dine in style, Eugene. I can make no promise of your future meals."

• • •

April 19, 1849

Dear Sister,
I am writing this on the canal, and we
have just left a tunnel. I had to stop
writing while we passed through. We

have been on this canal four days. Came across the Alleghany mountains by rail and were drawn up fifteen hundred feet, most of the way by ropes.

This is very bad writing. It is crowded here. There are three girls sitting directly in front of me. The boat is unsteady but not a worry. I know you can read these words, Hortense. For you can read anything in the shape of writing.

Tell Father that my courage is good. He must not listen to Mrs. Wyman at church. She thinks that anyone who goes to California would not be good for anything when they got back. Her idea is that any essence in a man drains out of him in the West. I shall prove her wrong. I have heard there are ten thousand at St. Louis and Independence that will cross the country. Mark my word when I say that I shall be one of them. Please do not worry about me. If I thought you did, I should not be able to enjoy myself.

I will mail this letter in Pittsburgh before I board there.

Your affectionate brother,
Eugene B. Chase

Chapter V

On the Way to St. Louis

Eugene walked back and forth on the riverboat deck, careful not to disturb the men already asleep. The fare from Pittsburgh to St. Louis cost nine dollars. He didn't have a cabin, only the stars above his head. The first day passed quickly. Most of the men played cards, their cigar smoke filling the air. Eugene was content to stand on deck. He had meant to open the diary. Now it was night. His writing must wait for morning.

The next day was warm and pleasant. He watched men at work along the river. Eugene thought of home. Calves were being born. His pony would hunger for oats. These memories made him want to write a letter.

The Ohio

Dear Hortense,
I hope you are able to read this. I am well.

37

I trust you are all well. I have much to tell
you about Uncle Lucien and the grand
house he is building. He is wonderful,
like I remembered him.
    And the life he leads –

Eugene stopped writing. Mention of Uncle Lucien
would never do. Father would hear the words and remember how his brother left Derby Line and never
returned. Eugene began again.

                              The Ohio
Dear Hortense,
I enclose a photograph taken on
bustling Broadway as it is called.
The picture is dark. Yet you can see
I am well. I have a Colt six-shot
revolver now. The Baby Dragon,
Uncle Lucien called it. Tell Enoch,
George, and Arthur to be good
boys. Tell Mother not to worry.
Ask Father to give my pony some
oats. I will write from St. Louis.

                    Your affectionate brother,
                              Eugene

Eugene sealed the letter. Then he picked up the diary

Hortense had given him.

> April 1849 – On my way to St. Louis.
> I've seen Uncle Lucien. I carry his revolver
> and his money with me. We made a deal.
> If I can return home with a clear one
> thousand dollars, I need not pay back
> even one dollar. What fine meals I ate
> with him. He would laugh at what I'm
> eating now. Beans and salt pork. Uncle
> Lucien said something I will never forget.
> "The fruits of the journey show in time.
> Remember that, Eugene."

Eugene had not started the next sentence before a small boy grabbed his pen. The boy dashed behind a young woman's full skirts.

"Joshua, give the gentleman his pen."

Eugene shaded his eyes with his hand. He wanted to see the young woman before him. Just then, the child peeked out from behind her skirts. Eugene reached for him. The boy cried with delight and handed back the pen.

"Joshua, be still," the young woman said.

"Is this your brother or your son?"

The young woman blushed. "My brother. I'm sorry he disturbed you. You looked involved in your writing."

Eugene put the diary in his coat pocket. "Come along," he said to the boy. "Let's give your sister a rest." Eugene lifted the boy onto his back. The child's pudgy fingers tightened around Eugene's neck.

Eugene ran up and down the deck. The boy laughed and shouted. The young woman smiled each time they ran past. She had dark curls beneath her bonnet and green eyes. She was as pretty as any girl Eugene had seen. Until he was out of breath Eugene didn't stop running. He returned the boy to his sister. The child kicked free and clung to Eugene again.

"What am I to do with him?" the girl cried.

Eugene looked down at the boy. "I think I have found a new friend. I'm Eugene Chase."

"Corinne Shaw," she answered. "This is Joshua Shaw."

In the evening Eugene took the diary from his satchel.

I have met a young woman. More
beautiful than any girl I've ever seen.
Her family boarded in Pittsburgh.
Her father has taken a church in
St. Louis. Corinne's brother is three.
He's taken a fancy to me. A lively
little fellow. His mother can't rest
for fear he will fall off the boat.

On the steamboat from Pittsburgh to St. Louis, Eugene met Corinne and her little brother, Joshua.

• • •

The next five days passed quickly. On the seventh day they reached Louisville. They were days behind what the captain had promised. There they boarded a steamboat called the *Cincinnati*.

"Do you think this boat is safe?" Corinne asked.

Eugene laughed. "One slap from the sea and she'd be gone."

Corinne tugged on her bonnet strings. "Do you think so, Eugene?"

"I'm teasing," he answered. Corinne was unlike Hortense. His sister would look at a steamboat and see a raft with an engine. She would know a raft held no power against a mighty river.

"Must you go to California, Eugene?"

He looked at Corinne. She was delicate and lovely. He would find no fairer in Derby Line.

"You could stay in St. Louis, Eugene. Father knows people. You could find work. Must you go?" Eugene saw that she was blushing.

"Joshua," she called. The boy was climbing the rail.

"Joshua," Eugene said. The boy heard Eugene's voice and climbed down.

Eugene wanted to say something to Corinne. She had asked him to stay. She had spoken of her feelings. Eugene said nothing.

"Mother will be looking for us, Joshua. Come along." Yet Corinne stood still. "Father says you're unwise. He thinks this gold rush is madness. He says there's evil in such a journey. I defend you to Father."

Joshua tugged at his arm. Eugene felt weak. There was an urge to say, "Yes, I will stay." Eugene touched the boy's head. "You, Joshua, must mind your sister."

•   •   •

Eugene's thoughts kept him awake that night. He heard noisy card games on the middle deck. On the lower deck he was alone. He looked at the river. There was only its blackness. Then in the distance he saw a fire.

The captain had passed Eugene earlier. The captain was a gruff man who spoke to almost no one. Eugene wanted to know about the fire. He caught up with the captain on the upper deck.

"Excuse me, sir. Can you tell me what's over there?"

The captain said nothing. Eugene waited. The question deserved an answer. Minutes passed. At last the captain spoke. "State prison is over there. Gets crowded and there's often a fire. Same on the river with boats." The captain paused. "We river men don't talk about fires. Tomorrow night we'll be in St. Louis.

I'd get some sleep, young man."

Eugene returned to the lower deck. He watched the fire. Then a bend in the river blocked the orange flames. The darkness returned.

Chapter VI

On Land Again

The next morning, Eugene heard shouts "Steamboat blew." He saw debris in the river and touched the thin wood railing. A steamboat loaded with cotton was like kindling. He understood why the captain had said river men did not talk about fires.

Just ahead of the *Cincinnati*, Eugene saw a steamboat easing its way toward the levee. One white man and several Negroes were on the riverbank. Eugene heard the *Cincinnati's* paddle begin to turn. They would not be stopping. Eugene wanted to get a better look at the men on the levee. None wore pants. The white man's shirt hung to his knees. There was something familiar about the way he stood, waving and shouting.

Eugene pushed his way to the stern. He had to see the man more clearly. Just then, the fellow began running along the levee. He cupped his hands and screamed. Eugene was certain he heard his name.

"Leal!" he shouted in return. "Leal!"

• • •

The *Cincinnati* headed up the river to St. Louis. Eugene lost sight of the boat with the survivors. Reverend Shaw came on deck. He held Joshua tightly by the hand. The boy remained quiet in his father's presence. Eugene told the Reverend what he had seen.

"Your friend must thank Almighty God for having saved him."

Eugene said nothing. He did not want to show disrespect. There was one thing Leal could do. He could swim. Leal would thank his summers in the river for saving him.

Reverend Shaw cleared his throat. "My daughter asked that I give this to you." He handed Eugene a letter. Eugene reached down and patted Joshua's head. By next week the boy would forget him.

"Thank you" he said to Reverend Shaw. Eugene opened the letter, saw Corinne's address, and a short note.

Eugene,
I must know of your safe arrival in
California. I ask that you write me
from there. May God protect you on
your journey.

Corinne

Eugene rolled up his bedding. He repacked his satchel. Then he stood on deck and waited. Enough of the river. Soon there would be land beneath his feet.

The *Cincinnati* reached St. Louis in the late afternoon. Eugene belonged to the land again. The St. Louis waterfront looked miles long. The steamboat carrying Leal might dock far away. Eugene took a last look at the *Cincinnati*. The Shaw family were still on deck. Eugene's arms were not free to wave good-bye unless he set his things down. He stood for a moment and looked at Corinne. She lifted Joshua to the rail. The child waved. Then Eugene turned and walked up the waterfront to find Leal.

• • • •

"I'm damn lucky, Eugene. Damn lucky." Leal paced the captain's cabin. Eugene sat and listened. He had boarded the steamboat and given Leal some clothes. Leal was three inches shorter than Eugene, twenty-pounds lighter and now resembled a boy.

"See this?" Leal held up a leather money belt. "Only condition Father would give me money. 'You wear a belt or else.' I've got money, Eugene. Lost everything else."

"You're alive. We'll buy supplies in California."

"Yeah, I'm alive. I need sleep and hot food."

"How many were saved?"

"Don't know. Don't much care. I'm alive. And we're going to California." Leal walked around the cabin, sat, then jumped to his feet. Eugene sat quietly. In the face of something awful, he was silent. Not Leal. Eugene remembered when Leal's mother had died six years earlier. Leal had talked often to Eugene, though he never mentioned his mother's death or the way he felt about it.

"We can sleep here tonight, Eugene. Captain won't make us leave. Other steamboats passed us by. Probably figured some darkies weren't worth the stop. I'm the only man wanted a boat to stop. The others took to the road."

"I'm lucky, Eugene. You know what the captain said? 'There's a fire, folks. No need to panic. Plenty of time to make shore.' About then, the boilers blew. You know how that sounds? I thought, hell. What's half a mile in strong currents for me? I dove in the river."

Leal sat down. "You see your uncle? You like New York City?" Eugene did not answer. Leal had fallen asleep.

• • •

48

St. Louis
April 29, 1849

Dear Hortense,
I'm in St. Louis. Leal is with me. I do
not wish to alarm you but his steamboat caught fire. I will say no more of
the accident. You will have the story
from Leal's father. I tell you the Mississippi is a river and no mistake.
You would think it a lake if you did not
know. It is from ½ to 3 or 4 miles wide,
with a very swift and strong current.
Few could swim it. It may well be
called "The Father of Waters." The
Ohio is a large stream but does not
compare with this.

    We have not missed our wagon
train. Our plan is to leave the first part
of May from Independence. We hear
there are 10,000 emigrants there. We
shall be among them.

    I would not back out now. Go
home to have people laugh at me.
They would say I had not spunk to
go through with what I undertake.
I hope you have sent letters to Fort
Kearny and Fort Laramie. Tell Father

49

and Mother I am well. I don't want
them to worry about me, for I think I
shall get along very well. I shall stay no
longer than I can for I shall want to see
you all so much. Tell Enoch, George and
Arthur to be good boys. I have not written
all I want to but shall write again before I
leave. Give my love to all and take a large
share of it yourself.

Your affectionate brother,
Eugene

Chapter VII

The Journey Begins

Independence Landing in Missouri was not much bigger than Derby Line. Where were all of the emigrants? Then a man pointed up the road. Independence City was three miles from the landing. Eugene and Leal walked toward it.

There the streets were filled. Thousands of men waited to go West. There were no hotel rooms and the courthouse had been opened to emigrants. Eugene found a spot to put his bedroll.

"How can I sleep on this damn hard floor?" Leal asked. He was edgy.

"Think how good the Plains will feel," Eugene said.

"Like hell," Leal said.

Eugene was filthy, but the bathhouse lines were long. He was hungry. The restaurant lines were even longer. The floor was hard. Yet sleep would ease discomfort. A day or two more and they would be headed West.

"We can't both sleep at the same time." Eugene handed Leal his pocket watch. "Wake me at midnight. I'll stay awake till morning."

When Eugene awakened, it was morning. Leal was asleep. Eugene sat up and checked his coat. His wallet was there. So was his revolver. But his satchel was gone.

"Looking for this?" a man said.

Eugene turned and saw a gray-haired man with the satchel. Eugene walked to where the man sat. "Thank you." He extended his hand. "Name's Eugene Chase."

"I know. I came to find you last night, Mr. Chase. That's when I saw a man eyeing your satchel. I heard you are traveling with the Pioneer Line. You're not attached to a company yet. That right?"

Eugene nodded. The man had a handsome face. High cheekbones. A gray moustache.

"What can you do?" the man asked.

Eugene laughed. "What can I do? Bake bread, boil coffee, shoot straight."

Eugene looked over at Leal and laughed again. "I keep watch without falling asleep. I might as well tell you. We don't have supplies."

"We don't need supplies," the man said. "We're overloaded. We're a train of men. None of the burdens

On the trail West, Eugene became friends with Judd, the doctor from Boston with a mysterious past.

of women. None of their graces, either. We're short two men. You interested, Mr. Chase?"

Eugene looked over at Leal.

"You need to talk it over with him?"

Eugene shook his head.

"You bake bread, Mr. Chase. You shoot straight. Man of few words, too. I heard your friend was on that steamboat. The one that burned below St. Louis."

"Leal's a good swimmer. Lucky, too."

"I think the company's complete." The man held out his hand. "Name's Judd."

Nine miles from Independence

Dear Hortense,
The journey West has begun. We're
camped on the prairie and expect to
move out tomorrow. All I see are the
white of tents and wagon tops. There
are smells of frying bacon and boiling
coffee. I wish Father could see this
earth. Rich and black. The grass is
lush. Wildflowers are everywhere.
You could fill every room in the
house. Early this morning, I walked
to a nearby creek. Wildrose, goose-
berries, and cornflowers were plenti-
ful. Later on, I'll not have a chance

for such walks. There will be danger
from Indians. Mother will hear this
and picture me dead from an arrow.
Two Indians came into camp yesterday.
One was painted. Leal lifted his rifle.
He is still nervous from the steamboat
fire. I think on the Plains he will forget
the river.

      I will mail this letter now. A
man in the company must return
to Independence. I promise to write
more often now. I am glad to be away
from city life. I am not a man who
could live with so many people.
As you well know, I like to be alone.
The Plains are a man's answer to
solitude.

      I think of home often. I should
like to ride my mare and feed her some
oats. I could make a whole meal out of
a cream pie. Yet I must forget these com-
forts. I long to see all of you very much.

      Your affectionate brother,
      Eugene

Chapter VIII

Campfire

The first few days on the Santa Fe Trail were difficult, the mules hard to handle. Men fought. In five days, they had made only forty miles.

The first days of walking left Eugene sore and weary. He had sat too long on the stagecoach, trains, and boats. The prairie grass soaked his pants to the hips. He slept in wet clothes.

They camped in late afternoon. Then the real work began. They formed circles and secured stock. The men who cooked gathered firewood. They got out supplies. The second week, Eugene was given sentry duty which meant less sleep.

Some nights the weather was kind and didn't pour rain. Then his company sat around the fire. There wasn't a fear of Indians yet. Ahead they had been warned of a tribe who liked to steal mules.

One evening as they sat by the fire Judd took out

his fiddle. Eugene knew little about him. Several times he had wanted to talk to Judd. Ask him his last name. Ask him where he was from. Yet something stopped him.

The men began to talk among themselves. Judd put down his fiddle and moved closer to the fire. Leal paced back and forth. He stopped behind Judd.

"Why's an old man like you going West?"

Eugene stiffened. Leal offended people. That's what Hortense said.

Judd didn't answer Leal. He picked up a stick and poked it in the fire. The other men stopped talking. Judd turned and looked at Leal.

"Been a townsman all my life, Leal. Had a longing for open land. Man shouldn't die with that longing."

Leal shrugged. "You're older than my father. He wouldn't go West."

Judd poked the fire's embers. Eugene watched them fly.

Judd spoke slowly. "We're born, Leal. We die. Our bones likely blow away. Doesn't mean we can't keep the fire going to the end."

"Bones and fires. What's that mean?"

Judd laughed. "You should know. You just outswam Death."

Leal stuck his hands in his pockets. "Don't know about that. I know one thing. I'm planning to get buf-

57

falo and a heap of gold."

A man behind Judd spoke. "Better learn to load the wagon first." All the men laughed. Leal shrugged and walked away.

Eugene remained by the fire. He poured himself a cup of coffee and braced himself. Without cream, he hated the bitterness of coffee. He reached up and rubbed his neck, felt a lump there.

Judd was watching him. "Something wrong, Eugene?"

Eugene shook his head.

"Are you after buffalo, Eugene. And a heap of gold?"

Eugene could see Judd's face in the firelight. He was smiling. Eugene stood. It was time to stand guard.

"You know, Judd. The prairie might strangle Leal. It's so damn quiet out here."

Eugene walked to where the mules were tied. He heard Judd laughing. Then everything was silent and dark.

Chapter IX

One Great, Moving Field

Eighty miles from Independence they reached the Kansas Cross.

A man named Thomas spoke. "Be the easiest cross we make."

Eugene looked across the river, watched two Indians row a ferry toward them. Thomas kept talking.

"Dollar a wagon. Worth every cent. Wait till we have to unload the wagons. Put the goods atop 'em. Just you wait."

Nothing cheerful arose from Thomas. Wagon wheels would sink in a prairie crevice. "You think that's bad? Wait till the next."

It was almost time to ferry their wagons. Each man in the company had to help. Leal wasn't around. Eugene reached down and felt the water. Not as cold as he expected. He looked up and down the river. Leal had gone for a swim. He would be one of the last to cross.

Eugene wet a handkerchief and tied it around his neck. What had began as a lump was now a boil. His collar rubbed it. He tried not to dwell on the pain. "We've come so many miles." He repeated the words aloud.

Yet the pain did not go away. Two nights later, Eugene couldn't eat. It hurt to chew. He left the campfire and stood before the prairie. Never had he felt anything so vast.

"Makes one feel small, doesn't it?"

Eugene turned. Judd stood behind him.

"Anything wrong?"

Eugene wished Judd would go back to the fire. He wanted to be alone. Judd didn't move.

"Got a boil on my neck. Hurts to chew," Eugene said.

"Wondered what the handkerchief was for. Come on over to the fire."

"Who has some clean rags?" Judd asked. One man rose and went to his wagon.

"We'll lance this in the morning," Judd said. Eugene didn't say anything. It hurt to talk.

"Had a carbuncle before?" Eugene shook his head. "It will hurt like hell." Judd folded a small square of cloth and secured it on a fork. He dipped the fork in boiling water and applied the wet mass to Eugene's neck. Eugene pushed his hands into the ground to keep from jumping up.

"This will bring it to a head. Hold on."

Judd dipped the cloth in boiling water again and again. He held it on Eugene's neck. At last he said, "That ought to do it."

The next morning Judd called Eugene to his wagon. He held a short, pointed knife in his hand.

"Hold this. Don't let go." Eugene held a bowl with both hands. He felt a swift cut. Pus poured into the bowl.

"Nasty carbuncle."

Judd applied a dressing to Eugene's neck. "We'll have to change this every day for a week. Keep your hands clean. You get one of these, you're likely to get more. You better bury that pus."

Eugene climbed down from the wagon. Judd shouted after him. "Don't wait to tell me next time."

• • •

June 3, 1849

Dear Hortense,
One never knows what to expect on
the Plains. Yesterday we had a heavy
hail storm. Three of the wagons blew
over and were damaged. The storm
came so hard we could not see six feet
in front. Hailstones as large as your

dumplings. But softer! During storms like these, we bed beneath wagons. A tent cannot withstand these winds.

The Plains are a great moving field. You can find angle worms out here as large as small snakes. Men get thirty to forty bushels of wheat to the acre. There are no stumps to pull and no rocky soil to plow.

You think I describe Paradise? Of course there isn't much wood. The major crop is grass. The wind wails across the empty landscape most days. Yet where can you get hailstones the size of dumplings? Tell Father I shall have enough of camping out by the time I return home.

I miss you all. I count on a letter at Fort Kearny. My health has never been better. Please take a walk in the forest for me. Smother your coffee in cream. And give my pony some oats.

Your affectionate brother,
Eugene

Chapter X

Some Walk, Some Ride

Eugene finished writing the letter. A woman had lost her husband three hundred miles out and come into camp that night. She offered to take mail in the morning. The woman, like many others, was headed East. Wagon trains had stock stolen. Women lost their men. Men lost their courage. They turned back. They gave up. More than once, Eugene wished he had gone to California by way of ship around Cape Horn. Each day grew more difficult. Eugene never thought of turning back. Men had begun to quarrel. One man was so lazy the company cut off his supplies. There was always work to be done. Leal was rarely around to do the work.

"Writing home?"

Eugene looked up when he heard Judd's voice.

"Just finished," he said.

"I've a favor to ask, Eugene. The woman over

there…" Judd pointed to her wagon. "She said a company lost mules last night. Not far from here. Leal's out there with twenty of our team. I take over at midnight."

"I'll go see how he is," Eugene said.

He put his letter in the wagon, then walked onto the prairie. Ahead he could see Leal's lantern. Eugene heard something. He quickly knelt in the grass. He heard something again. The same sound. A bird call?

He had his revolver. He could fire a shot. What if Indians were out there? What if mules had been cut loose? A shot would make things worse.

He didn't shout for help. He sang the song all 49ers knew. But he changed the words. Judd would hear them and understand.

> Oh, I've come from camp
> To see the mules,
> And what do you think I find?
> I'd like to say,
> But I'm afraid.
> Susanna, don't you cry.

He repeated the verse several times. He heard nothing but saw a lantern moving toward him.

"Judd?"

"What's wrong, Eugene?"

"Thought I heard something. Was afraid to fire.

*Eugene checked on Leal, who was supposed to be
standing guard over the company's team of twenty mules.*

Afraid I'd spook the mules."

They walked to where Leal lay sleeping. Judd shook his head.

"Let's check the mules."

They counted nineteen. One was missing.

"It wasn't your imagination. Damn him."

Judd shook Leal. "Some trains shoot sentries who sleep. Our company makes them walk."

Chapter XI

Fort Kearny

The men did not take kindly to news of the stolen mules. Leal walked beside the wagons. The men jibed at him. "You been wantin' to see Indians, Leal. Hell, you missed your chance." Eugene laughed along with the other men. Leal had brought ridicule on himself.

The wagons were within a day of Fort Kearny. Eugene hoped to find a letter there.

"You going to eat at the fort?" Judd asked that night.

"I'd like to. Depends on how much."

"I'll pay, Eugene."

"I couldn't have you do that."

"When a man offers to pay, you accept."

Fort Kearny had a few sod houses, a store and the frame of what was to be a hospital. One family cooked for the fort's officers. It was there travelers could take a meal.

Late in the afternoon, Eugene and Judd walked to the fort's store. There Eugene checked for mail. No letter from home. He tried to hide the bitterness he felt. Leal walked in and asked, "You eating here tonight?"

Eugene stared at the tea cannister on the counter. "I'm eating with Judd."

"Now, ain't that fine, Eugene?"

"Talk like you've always talked. Your family never said *ain't*."

"Thought I had a friend. Guess I figured wrong." Leal turned and left the store.

"How much for the tea?" Eugene asked.

"Two-fifty a pound," the storekeeper said.

"Two-fifty a pound. I'll forget drinking tea."

Eugene didn't know what pleased him more. Eating a home-cooked meal or sitting at a table. They were served ham, biscuits, and pie. Butter, molasses, and pickles were on the table.

Eugene and Judd ate and didn't talk. Eugene drank his coffee slowly. He watched the family's daughter as she waited tables. Leal and some men from another company came into the house. They sat across the room. The young woman went over to clear their table.

"You see my friend over there?" Leal spoke in a loud voice. The young woman looked in the direction Leal pointed.

"See his neck? Indian brave shot him." The young woman stared at Eugene. "An Indian squaw pulled the arrow out. She wanted Eugene for herself."

The men at Leal's table laughed. The young woman looked embarrassed and hurried away. Leal kept on talking loudly. "When Eugene left town, all the girls cried. They damn near flooded Derby Line."

Eugene finished his coffee. "Ready to go, Judd?"

"So long, Eugene," Leal yelled. "You leave that girl alone. You hear me?"

Judd paused outside the door and pointed to the store. "Wait a minute. I need something." He returned shortly with a small bundle.

They walked the half-mile to camp without talking.

"I think I'll turn in," Eugene said.

"Here." Judd tossed him the bundle. "Coffee's getting to my stomach. Thought we'd have tea."

The warm tea helped Eugene sleep. Yet at midnight, Thomas awakened him.

"You've got to get Leal. He took some guy's drinking bet. He's at the fort."

Eugene rose slowly. "Why didn't you bring him back, Thomas?"

"Hell, he ain't my problem."

Leal was so drunk he couldn't stand. A sentry helped Eugene drag Leal outside Fort Kearny. It was a half-mile to camp. Eugene lifted Leal onto his back.

Halfway he stopped and couldn't walk any farther. He dumped Leal onto the wet grass.

"Get up, Leal. I can't carry you anymore." He shook Leal, slapped his face, finally sat down.

Leal began to sob. He dropped his head into Eugene's lap. Eugene smelled vomit.

"So damn lovely. No trees. No nothing." Leal sat up. "There's cholera, Eugene. No one talks about it." He motioned to the fort. "They'll tell you different."

"I told 'em. We got no cholera. Not the Pioneer Line. They laughed. 'Count the graves, boy.'"

Leal grabbed Eugene's arm. "I don't want to die out here."

Eugene pulled his arm away. "Then don't drink."

"You've already got me in hell. Just like your father."

"This has nothing to do with church. Drinking won't make it any better. Can't you see that?"

Eugene put his arm around Leal's waist and helped him stand. "I won't be mocked, Leal. I want that understood."

Leal stumbled in the grass. "I drank too much. That's all. Won't happen again. I promise."

Chapter XII

Keeping a Promise

Eugene had hoped for a letter at Fort Kearny. He kept that hope alive until the wagon train left. Not receiving a letter made Derby Line feel farther away. Eugene began to worry about his family. Writing in his diary made home seem less distant.

> June 11 – Leal shot a buffalo today.
> The toughest, driest meat I ever ate.
> We gnawed on the buffalo meat at
> supper. Leal kept saying, "You like it?
> You like it?" Finally my friend Judd
> answered him. "Leal, I think you
> should have shot at something young
> and fat. Old bulls like me are too tough."
> Everyone laughed except Leal. Judd is
> better medicine than a doctor.

The days on the trail passed slowly. At last the Pioneer Line reached Ash Hollow. There was grass and fresh water. Firewood was easy to find. The companies rested and repaired wagons.

June 19 –We're stopping in Ash
Hollow. I washed my clothes today.
I wish Hortense and Mother could
see me. I draped my wet clothes on
bushes. Then Judd and I took a walk.
We thought we saw some wolves. We
couldn't be sure. I thought I heard a
baby pig. I had it roasted and eaten
until a yellow-headed bird sailed out
of a cedar. The bird squeaked and
grunted like a pig. Two Sioux passed
us by. One rode a coal-black pony.
They looked at us, then rode on.

June 21 – Men become what they are
on a journey like this. A man can't
pretend to be something he is not.
Lazy men are lazy. Complaining men
complain. Dishonest men cheat and
lie. Yet the good men far outnumber
the bad.

When the wagons left Ash Hollow, Eugene thought of

The trip from Independence to the gold fields of the West Coast took about five months at some twelve miles a day.

Fort Laramie. More than anything, he hoped for mail.
What he saw along the trail reminded him of home.
Rocking chairs, chests, anvils, chains.

June 24 – Why must men have so much?
I can't describe all we see along the trail.
We've been told to lighten our wagons.
Fort Laramie is only days ahead.

The Pioneer Line reached Fort Laramie at the
end of June. There was no mail for Eugene. That was
not the worst news.

June 25 – The gold has failed. Some men
said this rumor came from the East. They
said not to believe it. Other men buried
heads in their arms. Some even wept.
Thomas said he knew the gold
wouldn't last. Leal threatened to shut
Thomas up. Judd said nothing. Later I
asked him what he thought.
"Do you want to believe that, Eugene?
I told Judd, "No."
"Then don't believe it," he said.

June 29 – No more than sixty days going
from here. That's what we're told.
Tomorrow we're having a general turnout.

All baggage will be weighed. The Pioneer Line pilot wants to make sure nothing gets smuggled in. I've stopped eating meat. It doesn't agree with me. I just crumble hard bread in my tea. How I would like to eat at home. I think I would enjoy supper more than before.

Chapter XIII

Independence Rock

Eugene walked beside the wagons. He thought of the Sweetwater River ahead. Mountain trails. Poisoned springs. Broken wagons. They had come fifty of the worst miles.

The train stopped. A cry came from the front to camp for the night. Eugene looked several wagons back and saw Leal. Eugene was tired of listening to him. He was weary of seeing cholera graves and things thrown from wagons. The Platte Valley was lined with graves and discarded things.

Eugene heard Leal call his name. But he walked ahead to see Judd.

"So much for the Sweetwater."

Judd leaned out from his wagon. "We'll be past this awful stretch tomorrow."

As Judd spoke, Leal burst around the wagon.

"Independence Rock is ahead. A man in the rear

company's getting some mules."

Leal moved his feet while he talked. Eugene tried to remember if Leal ever stood still. He either moved his feet or moved his mouth.

"Help me out. Cook tonight."

"When don't I help you out?"

Leal grinned. "Sure beats the old Platte. I'll carve my name on Independence Rock. Want me to carve yours?"

Eugene turned away and didn't answer. There was firewood to gather, a fire to build, bread to bake, coffee to boil. "Damn," he muttered.

"Want some help, Eugene?"

Eugene looked up at Judd and saw a small grin on his face. "No," he said. "I don't want any help."

Eugene grabbed a gunny sack and an axe. At least he didn't have to care for the stock or stand guard duty tonight.

At a short distance from the camp Eugene came across a bookcase. He laughed aloud. It had been left standing. He felt like pushing it over. He walked around the bookcase and there in the shadow, he saw a snake coiled to strike.

Eugene raised his axe. Just then the snake rolled over and played dead. A hognose. Eugene had heard stories about this snake. Threatening but harmless. He laughed again.

Eugene walked another few yards and found an

open chest. He broke the chest into pieces and filled his gunny sack. There were thunderclouds above. He walked quickly toward the camp. The sack's weight kept him from running.

Eugene was close to camp when the downpour hit. He pulled the sack between his legs and knelt. He held his coat over his head. The rain ran off all around him. Several men crawled under the wagons when the rain hit. They shouted at Eugene. Some were laughing.

Nothing seemed funny. Then he remembered that Leal was up ahead on Independence Rock. Maybe he would get washed off, along with his name. Eugene began to laugh, louder than the rain.

That evening the sky dumped rain for hours. Eugene served hard bread and cold coffee in tents and under wagons. Leal had not returned. The rain finally stopped. Eugene built a fire and sat beside it. Judd came out from his wagon. He sat down, took some kindling in his hands, tore twigs in half.

"Are you your brother's keeper, Eugene?"

"Why do you ask?"

"Because I'm leaving the train at Carson River. The line's short on supplies. We're short on time, too."

"What do you mean?"

"The early snow in the Sierras. I hear some trains got trapped last winter. We can make the last two hundred miles on foot. I'd like you to join me, Eugene. I don't want Leal. Do you understand?"

Eugene nodded and said nothing. At last Judd rose. He shook his legs.

"I liked what you did this afternoon."

Eugene smiled. He'd forgotten to tell Judd about the snake.

"What did you like?"

"The way you laughed out there in the rain. The last fifty miles have brought out the worst in a lot of men. Not in you. Think about Carson River."

Judd walked to his wagon. Eugene stayed by the fire. His wet coat hung nearby. The coat would be damp in the morning. His bedroll wasn't wet. The thought of dry warmth led Eugene to the wagon. Tomorrow he would see the Sweetwater. He heard another downpour begin. Beneath the wagon, he was warm and dry.

Sometime later, Eugene awakened, saw nothing but darkness. He felt water dripping on his face, heard a voice.

"I carved your name on Independence Rock."

Eugene grabbed at the darkness.

"What the hell?"

Eugene threw himself over Leal, pushed his shoulders down. He saw white teeth in the darkness.

"You get water on my bedding again, I'll –"

"Shut up," someone shouted.

Leal didn't move. Eugene smelled liquor on his breath. "I'm not your keeper. Do you hear me? I'm not your keeper."

Eugene crawled into his bedroll. Leal lay beside him, uncovered.

Chapter XIV

Digging for Roots

Eugene awakened the next morning. Leal had crawled to the far end of the wagon and covered himself with a blanket.

After breakfast, the trains were ready to leave. Eugene walked over to the wagon where Leal lay sleeping.

"We're moving out. You've got to get up."

Leal didn't answer

Eugene crawled under the wagon. Leal had thrown off the blanket. "Get me some water," he whispered.

Eugene slid out from under the wagon.

"What's wrong?" Thomas asked.

"Leal's sick."

"Too much liquor?"

"I suppose," Eugene said.

Leal drank only a little of the water, then vomited. A stream of bile poured from his mouth. Eugene took his handkerchief and wiped the yellow-green vomit off Leal's neck. In doing so, he felt Leal's warm face.

Eugene called to a few men outside the wagon. "Let's move him inside. He's got to ride today."

That day the wagons passed Independence Rock. They passed Devil's Gate and the Sweetwater River. Several times Eugene climbed into the wagon. He found Leal asleep. He thought by evening Leal would be better. His sickness was nothing more than too much liquor. By evening, Leal's fever was higher. He refused the food Eugene offered him.

"Everyone said it was the liquor. But he won't swallow anything. He's burning up."

"I'll look at him," Judd said.

Eugene climbed into the wagon with Judd. He watched as Judd unbuttoned Leal's shirt, felt under his arms, examined his palms.

"What's the matter, Leal?"

Leal didn't answer. Judd raised his voice. "What's wrong?"

"Get out," Leal cried. "Leave me alone."

Judd motioned to Eugene. They jumped down from the wagon.

"He could have cholera," Eugene said.

"It's not cholera."

"How do you know, Judd? We know it's all

around us. Leal's with men from other companies all the time. He could have caught it."

"It's not cholera. His voice is good. His skin's not blue."

"How do you know about cholera?"

"I spent over thirty-five years doctoring people, Eugene. I tell you, Leal doesn't have cholera. It's a bad case of influenza."

Eugene looked at Judd. He suddenly understood. The surgical knife, Judd's manner of speaking.

"I'm sorry, Judd."

"Sorry about what? I'm going West to mine gold. That doesn't mean I wouldn't help a sick man. We need water and rags. Brew tea. Find some sugar."

• • •

Eugene sat with Leal all evening. Again and again he climbed from the wagon. He tossed out warm water, replaced it with cold. He spooned sweetened tea into Leal's mouth. After midnight, Judd came to the wagon.

"I'll take over until morning."

"You don't have to do that."

"I don't have to. I can't see you getting sick. Can't be nursing two men."

Eugene didn't argue. He needed to sleep. He felt ill from the poor food. He no longer ate any meat. His gums had begun to bleed. His teeth were loose. He couldn't eat bread without soaking it in tea.

Through the South Pass and the Sublettes Cut-off, Leal rode in the wagon. Eugene and Judd took turns feeding him. They sponged him down. They sat up nights with him. Finally Leal was able to walk beside the wagons. Yet he was withdrawn, wept openly, spoke to no one except Eugene.

"I'll never make it across the desert."

Eugene heard what Leal said and felt no sympathy. Leal had ridden in the wagon during the worst part of the journey.

"I guess you'll make it across the desert. Or you'll die."

"I should never have left Derby Line. I should have turned back after that fire."

"Damn your *shoulds*, Leal.'

•　　•　　•

The Pioneer Line finally reached the Humboldt River. Eugene had expected the final three hundred miles to California to be easier. He thought the worst was behind them. All those miles of suffering. The heat and sandy trails. The dust that made it impossible to see.

The Humboldt River wasn't any better. It was cold by night, hot by day. There were swamps, which meant grazing was risky for the mules. Each day was harder than the last.

One morning, Judd stopped Eugene after break-fast. "How are your teeth?"

"About to fall out of my head."

"You've been eating bread too long. The line's getting short of supplies. We tossed too much at Fort Laramie. We don't have enough to see us through. I figure another week. Then we'll leave the train. Have you told Leal?"

"No, but I will, in my time."

Judd gave Eugene a pat on the back. "What do you say we find ourselves an Indian today?"

Eugene stared at Judd. "Why do you want to find one of these diggers?"

"Because they live off this miserable land. They dig what they need out of the ground. And they survive. They know what to eat."

Judd reached into his pocket and took out a pocket knife. "You've got loose teeth. I've got a bad stomach. One of these local Indians can help us."

The train made camp early that day. Judd and Eugene set out. They carried rifles and circled a mile from camp. After an hour, they spotted someone. He saw them but didn't stop his work. Judd walked over and knelt down. The Indian lifted roots from the ground and placed them on a tattered cloth. As he dug up a large root, he raised his head and grinned.

Judd took the knife from his pocket. The Indian watched Judd open the blades. Then Judd set the knife on the ground and held up one finger. He placed his hands on his stomach and pretended to vomit.

The Indian nodded. Judd held up two fingers. He pointed to Eugene.

"Show him your teeth."

Eugene opened his mouth and pushed against his spongy gums. He tasted blood as it ran down his throat. The Indian gathered the roots and tied his cloth. He motioned for them to follow him.

"You think he understands?" Eugene said.

"He understands. I just hope he doesn't lead us too far from camp. He might like to have our rifles more than the knife."

They walked a good mile. The man stopped. He picked some leaves off a bush. Then he knelt and blew through his hands, as if to start a fire. He made a motion of stirring something. He drank it. He pointed to Judd's stomach.

They walked another mile and stopped. He dropped to the ground and dug around. He lifted out some bulbs. He raised one to his mouth and pretended to chew it. He pointed to Eugene.

Judd held out the pocketknife. The Indian took the knife and went back to digging in the ground. Eugene and Judd walked away.

"Can we trust him?"

"I trust him," Judd said. "I've been thinking. After I mine, I'd like to see what I can learn from these

Judd traded a pocket knife to a Pawnee Indian who showed him which roots and bulbs would cure his and Eugene's ills.

Indians."

"About medicine? What could they tell you?"

"They know things I never learned in books. When you get too far from nature, there's trouble. I guess that's why I worried about dying a townsman."

Eugene waited. Judd said nothing more. He didn't say if he had a family in the East. He didn't say where he lived. Eugene asked no questions.

That night, Judd boiled the leaves in water and drank the tea. Eugene cut a bulb into pieces. He chewed as many pieces as he could.

"I hope this does something for my gums. Sure smells awful. What do you think it is?"

Judd laughed. "I don't know. But my stomach feels better already."

Eugene had doubts but continued to eat the bulbs. When the train reached the Humboldt Sink, Eugene's gums had stopped bleeding. He could eat hard bread again.

Chapter XV

The Desert

The Humboldt Sink was worse than the Humboldt River. There was no escaping the smell of death. The remains of dead animals lay everywhere. All the men in the Pioneer Line had been told to cut hay. It was needed to get the mules across forty miles of desert.

"Can it be as bad as everyone says?" Eugene asked Judd. They were piling hay into the wagons.

"We take as much water and hay as we can. We rest tonight and tomorrow. Beyond that we take it mile by mile."

After supper, Leal took Eugene aside. "I'll never make it across the desert. You've got to talk Judd into letting me ride. The other men won't argue with him."

Eugene pulled his arm away. "You'll walk like the rest of us."

"I'm too weak."

89

"No weaker than anyone else. You were sick. Now you're not. The mules don't need your weight."

"You've changed, Eugene."

"I've changed, yes. You haven't. I'll tell you something, Leal. If you can't make it across the desert, you'll never be able to mine. You've got to dig for gold."

"Why don't you shut up," Leal shouted. "I'm sick of your high talk. You've gotten it from him." He pointed toward Judd's wagon.

"I've known you all my life, Leal. I hate to see it end like this."

"End like what?"

Eugene didn't answer. He walked away from the fire and stood in the darkness. The desert was out there. It had to be crossed. One mile at a time.

The next afternoon, the wagon train left.

Only the drivers rode. The wagons had been loaded with hay and water. Eugene wore a canteen around his neck. When he wanted water, he would wait one hour. The way to get across the desert was to resist impulse.

The wagons moved into the night. The men walked as quickly as they could. At midnight they stopped to feed the mules. With the sun down, Eugene felt no thirst. The full canteen hung from his neck. In the first ten hours, the wagon train covered twenty-five miles. Then they hit the sand. The mules struggled to plod through it. Eugene tried not to think about fifteen miles of sand. He tried not to think about daylight. Now, darkness was a friend.

When daylight came, they rested. They boiled coffee and ate bread. Eugene needed sleep more than food. When it came time to leave, Leal wasn't there.

Eugene shouted. "Where's Leal? Look in the wagons until you find him."

Leal crawled from a wagon when he heard the shouting. No one spoke to him. The silence was punishment enough.

"We should have started earlier yesterday," Judd said to Eugene. "We'll hit the worst part at midday."

Eugene didn't answer. His lips were caked with dried saliva. He looked at his watch. He would drink water at 11 o'clock. Only one small sip.

Sweat ran off Eugene's back into his pants. He took off his hat. He tied a handkerchief above his eyes. The sweat burned them. At 11 o'clock, Eugene took one sip of water. The small taste made his thirst worse. He plugged the top of his canteen.

"You got water, Eugene?" Leal asked.

"Where's your water?"

Leal held up his empty canteen.

By noon with the sun overhead, the men and mules began to fail. The call came to water the stock.

"We're making a mile an hour, at most." Eugene turned and saw his friend. Judd was forty years older than Eugene. For the first time, Eugene saw his age.

"What is it, Eugene?"

"Nothing. You have water?"

"Enough to see me to the Carson River." Judd was leading the mule, not riding in the wagon.

Within minutes, a hand grabbed Eugene's shirt. "Slow up. I can't make it." Leal fell into the sand. Eugene waved the canteen above his head.

"One more hour, then we both get a drink. But don't talk to me. Not one damn word. You understand?"

So they walked and sank. An hour more. One more mile. "Here," Eugene said at last. "Two small sips. Enough to wet your mouth and throat. Don't make me pull it away. Or you'll have no more."

Leal drank from the canteen. If Judd had figured right, they would be at the Carson River by 5 o'clock. Three more hours.

Wherever Eugene looked, he saw signs of death. Abandoned wagons. Remains of mules, horses, and oxen. Piles of bones dried in the sun.

"I can't lift my feet," Leal cried.

"You didn't come this far to quit."

At 3 o'clock, he and Leal drank from the canteen again.

Eugene looked back, saw Judd and his mule toward the rear of the company. He was alone. Judd had put distance between himself and other men. Eugene knew to respect it.

He shook the canteen. Hardly any water left. Not enough for two more drinks. What if Judd had been wrong? What if another six miles lay ahead? The men would be drinking mule blood.

At 4 o'clock, Eugene handed the canteen to Leal. Just then, he heard shouts from the forward wagon. The cry came all along the train. "It's ahead. The Carson River. They can see her trees."

Eugene closed his eyes. He breathed deeply. Then he straightened up and opened his eyes. He brushed the sand and grit from his face. He handed Leal the canteen. "Finish it," he said.

When they reached the Carson River, the men put their hands in the clean water. Some drank until they vomited. Many men wept.

Eugene saw Judd sitting on the bank of the river. His head was on his knees. Eugene looked in the other direction. He saw a grove of cottonwood trees and walked toward them. The ground felt firm and solid.

He lay beneath the trees, watched the flat, silver leaves move in the breeze. He listened. The trees were calling to him. *Eugene. Eugene.* He turned over and shut his eyes. He wept with a joy he had never known.

Eugene stayed under the cottonwood trees until the sun set. He heard little noise from camp. It had been almost thirty-six hours since anyone had slept. And fifteen hours since they had eaten. He walked

After crossing forty difficult miles of desert terrain, members of the company reached the Carson River.

slowly toward the camp. He found Judd seated by a fire.

"How are you?" Eugene asked.

Judd sighed. "Never more tired in my life. You and I have two hundred miles to go. We'll rest tomorrow and leave the next day. I want my pick in the ground before October first."

Eugene saw a shadow move across the fire. Judd stood. "Good night Eugene. Good night, Leal."

"What's he talking about?" Leal asked.

"Judd and I are leaving the train."

"What about me?"

"This is where we part, Leal."

"You don't mean that, Eugene."

"You're not a man I can work with."

"You'd leave a friend. Just like that?"

"Not just like that. I saw you through the worst. I'd be no friend to carry you any farther."

"It's Judd. Damn him."

"No, Leal. It's me. Understand that."

Leal sank down by the fire. Eugene walked to the riverbank. He put his face in the clean water and drank until he could hold no more. There were only two hundred miles between the river and his dream.

Chapter XVI

Weaverville

September 20, 1849

Dear Hortense,
On April 20 I wrote from St. Louis. Now
five months to the day, I am in California.
I will write in haste. We have just arrived
in Weaverville. The mail goes out the first
of the month. Then no mail leaves until
November.

I have not in any other letter told you
the worst of this journey. I feared that Mother and Father would worry. I left the Pioneer Line at Carson River after we crossed
the worst stretch of desert known to man.
A doctor named Judd also left the train. I
know little of Judd's past. Yet I will tell you
he is the finest man I have ever known.

What you heard in the East about
the Pioneer Line is true. There were some
forty deaths from cholera. But there was
no cholera in the company I was with. By

the time we reached the Humboldt, supplies were gone. There was much hunger.

I have not mentioned Leal. I do not know if he will mine gold or not. I do know he is not a man I can work with. Leal and I parted ways at the Carson River. I think you at home will say among yourselves, "We could have told Eugene this." I hope you have the kindness to say nothing. Mr. Hill is our neighbor. My hope is that Leal makes it home safely. Men's natures are revealed on a journey. I had to make the journey to know the truth of this.

The last stretch of mountains was hard on Judd. His age is not in his favor. And mining, we are told, is the hardest work of all. I am going to stick a little piece of gold on a wafer inside so that you can may see how it looks.

Take comfort, Hortense. I am well and hearty. My spirits have never been better. I promise to write often. Address your letters in care of the Independent Mail Express in Sacramento, California.

Your affectionate brother,
Eugene

Chapter XVII

No Regrets

Eugene and Judd reached Hangtown in late September. They had one mule and a few supplies. "We need to find an old miner who likes to talk," Judd said.

The following morning they met Henry. They saw him sitting on a stump of wood, feeding his burro.

Henry laughed and slapped his knee when Judd and Eugene started asking questions. "You got more questions than a frog's got croaks. Well, sit down and have some breakfast."

Henry picked up the burro's bowl. He wiped it with a rag and then mixed flour and water in it. He poured the flapjack batter in a pan.

"Father and son come to make a fortune. Ain't that right?"

"Two sons," Judd said.

Henry laughed. He flipped the flapjacks. He

handed a plate of them to Eugene. "Molasses is right over there."

Eugene started to spoon molasses over his flapjacks. The jar was full of black ants.

"Dig in, young fellow. You don't get free breakfast in town."

Eugene watched Judd spoon molasses over his flapjacks and pick ants off his plate.

Henry handed each of them a cup of coffee as thick as mud. Eugene glanced about the camp. Henry had a brush shanty. Eugene saw a cot just inside the door. The blankets were caked with mud. Dust was everywhere.

"Want some beans?"

Eugene saw a pot of beans by the fire. They were covered with scum. Eugene felt his stomach weaken.

"Is there much stealing here?" Judd asked.

"Couple of men got hanged last winter. Lynch law. There ain't much trouble. I keep my pistol and Bowie knife handy just in case."

Eugene and Judd sat with Henry most of the morning. He showed them what they needed to buy and told them how to stake a claim.

On October first, Eugene and Judd swung their picks into the ground. Eugene thought back to the rocky soil in Vermont. It was soft compared to this ground. Having to dig down three or four feet didn't help either. Eugene saw the strain in Judd's face.

They loosened the ground with their picks. With their spades they tossed dirt in the wheelbarrow, then wheeled it to the river. There they dumped the dirt into a cradle.

Mining for gold wasn't like any work Eugene had ever done. He had never stood in an icy river. He had never rocked a cradle. It sounded easy, like something a mother did. But the cradle held a pile of dirt and it had to be rocked until all the dirt dissolved. Then a thin layer remained. That layer had to be washed and rewashed. Finally, the gold separated from the dirt.

When Eugene first saw the gold, he laughed. He sat down by the side of the river. Mud and leaves stuck to his wet pants. He couldn't stop laughing.

"What is it, Eugene?" Judd asked.

"Look." Eugene held out the pan. There were specks of gold. "Leal expected nuggets the size of a fist. If he's mining, he's sure disappointed. Folks at home see us picking up gold the size of rocks. What do we find? Grains of sand."

Eugene and Judd worked their first claim for ten days. Then they cashed in their gold. Eugene sat down in the dusty street of Weaverville and took out his diary. He did some calculations. They had paid seven dollars each for a room. Board had cost another three dollars. That came to $200. They spent $100 on supplies. Their claim had brought in $400. Which meant they had cleared $100.

Eugene had never been so tired. He had never eaten so much bad food. He had never slept in such a lumpy bed. He had never been so dirty. And he had made five dollars a day. Fifty dollars. Eugene sat in the dust in Weaverville and laughed. Maybe it wasn't so awful to be a fool.

Later that day, Henry didn't laugh "You made your room and board," he said. "You bought supplies, too. What the hell are you complaining about? Everybody talks about the big strike. Nobody talks about the fellow who can't pay his board. By next year, it'll be worse. There will be more miners. Higher prices. Nobody will make board."

The months passed in Weaverville. The cold, wet weather arrived. Dreams of gold turned to mud. Eugene suspected that Judd welcomed the winter days. Darkness came early. They worked less. They were making enough money to keep ahead of their board. Now Eugene saw ways to make more money.

"We'll build a shed in Hangtown. We'll stock up on supplies. In spring, we can rent the shed and move on."

They built the shed and bought a barrel of flour. During the rainy season they mined when they could. The other days they sat in their shed and waited for spring.

One day Judd pushed his plate of food away. He ate nothing. Eugene noticed he was thinner. He had begun to cough. One evening Eugene felt a yearning for butter.

"My mother's butter would sell for two dollars a pound here. I can see her larder. Each pound of butter looks like gold. Mining isn't the only way to make money. I'd like to haul. Build more sheds. Sell my sister's pies." Eugene looked over at Judd. He expected him to laugh. Judd had fallen asleep.

"How's Judd?" Henry asked the following day.

"Not good. But he has time to rest before we leave."

"He seen a doctor?"

Eugene laughed. A prince wouldn't be a prince in Hangtown, he thought.

"Henry," Eugene said. "Judd *is* a doctor."

• • •

That winter, Eugene kept their mining accounts in his diary. On long days when rain fell, Judd slept. Eugene thought about the journey West and wrote in his diary. It made home seem less far away.

"Did I tell you about Corinne?" Eugene said one afternoon.

Judd raised himself on one arm and smiled. His cheeks were hollow. The flesh beneath his neck hung loosely. "Who's Corinne?"

"Girl I met on the river."

"Any regrets you came West, Eugene?"

"No regrets."

Judd rose from his cot. He walked slowly to the door. He stood in the doorway and looked out. "We need a new mule, Eugene. That fellow came all this way. He's worn out."

"We can get a mule for under two hundred dollars. In another month, the rain will stop. We'll be able to leave. I listen to the miners a lot. I've heard of good places up north."

Eugene looked at Judd. He wasn't listening.

"You have some paper, Eugene?"

That afternoon, Judd lay on his cot and wrote. In the evening he gave Eugene a letter.

The following morning Eugene mailed Judd's letter. It was addressed to Mrs. Sarah McCloud, in Boston, Massachusetts.

Chapter XVIII

Letter from Hangtown

Eugene awakened early the last day in February.

"Judd," he called. "You getting up?" There was no answer.

"The time's come to buy the mule. We're going to find good diggings this spring. I know it. We ought to leave next week. Will you be rested by then?"

Judd raised himself just off the cot. "The diggings haven't mattered, Eugene. You know that."

Eugene walked to the doorway and hesitated. "I won't be long."

"Take your time," Judd said. Then he laughed. "And don't pay over a hundred and fifty for that mule."

Eugene smiled when he heard Judd's laughter. "I promise. Not a dollar more. You haven't been eating much lately. I'll get some soup at a boardinghouse."

Judd swung his legs to the floor and sat up. "You're a fine young man, Eugene Chase."

Eugene opened the shed door. Sunlight flooded the entrance. Eugene felt something heavy rise from his chest to his throat. There was so much he wanted to say to Judd. He hesitated in the doorway.

"I'll be back soon. Get some rest."

Judd raised his hand in farewell. "Good-bye, Eugene," he called.

Eugene found the mule he wanted in Hangtown. He stopped to buy soup at a boardinghouse.

From outside the shed, he called to Judd. "Come see our new mule." There wasn't an answer. He glanced inside. Judd had let the fire go out. Eugene led the mule to the rear of the shed and opened the stall. The other mule was gone.

Darkness came early in February. With only one window in the shed there was little light. Eugene walked over to Judd's cot. On it he found a note.

> The old mule and I have journeyed on.
> We're going to find an Indian for what
> ails us. I know you'll understand. Good
> luck with the diggings.
>
> Judd

Eugene stood in the doorway until dark. With the darkness came rain. Eugene walked over to Judd's cot and sat down. The rain continued all night. In the morning, Eugene was alone. Judd had not returned.

He had put a distance between himself and other men. Eugene knew to respect it.

It rained all day. Mud seeped under the doorway. Sun or rain, Eugene decided to leave Hangtown the next day. He took his pen and paper from his leather pouch.

March 1, 1850

Dear Hortense and family,
This may well be my last letter for some
time. Tomorrow I move on to better diggings farther north. Mother and Father,
do not worry. My spirits are good, as is
my health. I want you all to know I do
not regret having come to California. It
is a hard country to live in. Yet I should
not have been satisfied if I had not made
the journey. Mining is hard work, but
you are your own master. You get your
pay each night. Be it one dollar or
twenty-five.
    If the spring diggings are good, I
will be home by early winter. I have
traveled the Plains. I have crossed the
mountains. I have walked the desert.
I will return by way of the sea. If I
can make my passage home and a clear

After mining gold, Eugene returned to Derby Line, Vermont and was able to build the house he lived in until his death.

thousand, I will be content. I long to
see all of you very much.

Your affectionate brother and son,
Eugene

Eugene sealed the letter and sat quietly for a time. Then he walked to the doorway and listened to the rain. Tomorrow he would journey deep into the mountains in search of new diggings. By early summer he would have his thousand dollars. Of that he was certain.

He leaned in the doorway of the shed in Hangtown. He listened carefully. He could hear the sound of water hitting the sides of a sailing ship. He could smell the sea air. He looked toward the horizon. He watched for land. Eugene knew he was almost home.

Epilogue

That evening in the mountains when I finished reading Eugene B. Chase's last letter, I felt sad. My great-great grandfather had spoken to me and become part of my life. Yet I didn't know the end of his story. Had he made his thousand dollars and returned to Derby Line? My grandfather Eugene, the person who knew the story, was deceased. His sister Kathleen, my great aunt, was alive, though she avoided talking about her life. She and her brother Eugene had been orphaned in early childhood. Their father, Peter McLaren, a Scottish immigrant, had died when Eugene was a boy and Kathleen a baby. Their mother Kathleen later remarried a wealthy man from California named Chester Smith. Eventually, despite an illness, she had taken the children by train from New York to California. Soon after, gravely ill, she died in Los Angeles. The children were living with their stepfather's elderly parents at the time. Then Chester Smith lost the family's money and shot himself in a Los Angeles bank one day. A painful story, which suggested why

Aunt Kathleen did not appreciate questions about the past.

Yet that night in the mountains something strange happened as I sat in bed listening to the creek. A clipping fell from the back of the ledger where there were empty pages. It was a news article, badly yellowed with age. It described the stone house that Eugene built in Derby Line with the money he had earned in California. I also learned that he died in Derby Line, Vermont in 1894, at age sixty-five.

What has kept my great-great grandfather alive for me? The voice in his letters.

The story I've told is fictional, by which I mean an act of imagination. I do not know the name of the young woman that Eugene met on the river boat. I only know from a letter that he was taken with her. He might have stopped his journey West for her. I also don't know the name of the young woman's brother. From Eugene's letters I sensed he had a way with children. I do know that Eugene had a conflict with a friend from home and they parted ways. Leal is that character. Conversations that Eugene shared with his sister, Hortense, are unknown. But I sensed a deep affection between them, and every letter was addressed to her. And the older man who positively influenced Eugene's journey West? Judd is my reflection of that man.

My imagination created situations and characters from my great-great grandfather's letters. My imagination did not create the underlying emotions. I tried to be faithful to the feelings Eugene Chase expressed. He was sensitive to both people and nature. The world around him on his journey West was often brutal and violent. His gentle nature prevailed. He did, however, change in other ways. By journey's end the voice in the letters is clear and resolute. It is the voice of a man. The boyish parts of himself lay scattered along the Gold Rush trail.

"I must go West," Eugene told his family. And so he left, going from the known to the unknown, from the certain to the uncertain. And as Uncle Lucien told him they would, the fruits of his journey revealed themselves in time.

I thank my great-great grandfather for his letters, which helped me leave a place I deeply loved. Eugene's voice was with me as I lived and adapted to five foreign countries and places within the United States.

That summer of 1979, my great-great grandfather's voice spoke to me from 1849. One hundred thirty years later, the journey he recounted in his letters rekindled a fire in my spirit. His voice gave me the courage to move on, knowing that I carried his roots with me.

Eugene's Gallery

From the time of my great-great grandfather's overland journey in 1849 from Vermont to California, it goes without saying that life has changed dramatically. Many of the things Eugene B. Chase mentioned in his letters and diary are unfamiliar to us now. This gallery is to help readers understand what Eugene experienced on the trail and while mining for gold in northern California

Right: *The actual letter that Hortense wrote to her brother, Eugene. You can see on the top left that the envelope is postmarked Derby Line, Vermont, and simply addressed to "Mr. Eugene B. Chase, San Francsico, California." Below the envelope is the first page of Hortense's letter to her brother.*

Derby Line Sept 17th 1849

My Dear Brother Eugene

It is Monday morning. and there is
a lot of work to do, but the steamer, Empire
City, has just come in from Chagres and
will soon return, and we wish this letter
to go in it. we have written several letters
too San Francisco. but do not know whether
you will receive them or not. but hope
you have. as they would do you a
great deal of good. A week ago we received your letter which was written at
Fort Larimie. It was a long time coming
but you cannot imagine how glad we
were to get it. We had not heard from
you for so long, that we were feeling very
bad. but that informed us of your safe
arrival there. and I think by this time
if you had good luck you must be
in the "diggins". Now I want to caution
you if you are there not to work too
hard. I hope your health continues as
good as when you wrote, at the same
time with yours come a letter from
Sell. and one from William Station. he
was a few days behind you. and in
hopes to overtake you in a short time

113

Eugene made good on the promise that he would return home to Derby Line, Vermont and build a house with the money he earned in the California gold fields. As you can see on the map below, Derby Line, Vermont is situated directly on the border dividing the United States from Canada. The actual border runs under the town's library.

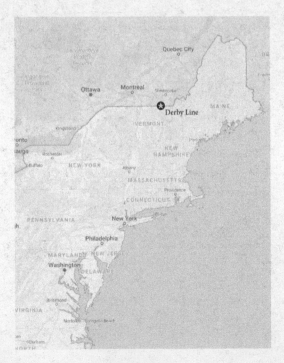

Above: *Riverboats were a popular mode of transportation in the mid-1800s, especially on the major rivers of the Midwest and Far West. Relatively flat-bottomed, they could navigate in shallow waters. They were typically propelled by large paddlewheels at the stern, powered by wood-fired steam engines. Most riverboats had twin smokestacks belching smoke, steam, and cinders.*

Above: *Situated on the western bank of the Mississippi River, St. Louis, Missouri was a thriving city in the mid-1800s and the fourth largest in the country.*

Above: *The covered wagon evolved from a standard wooden farm wagon. Overland migrants fitted the farm wagons with metal bows, over which they stretched canvas, thus creating a cover. Because the canvas reminded some travelers of sails, covered wagons were sometimes called "prairie schooners."* Below: *Making the most of a small amount of space: the typical arrangement of family possessions and supplies in a covered wagon.*

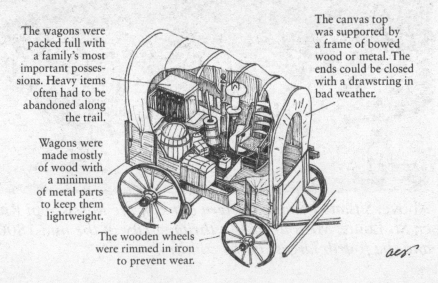

The wagons were packed full with a family's most important possessions. Heavy items often had to be abandoned along the trail.

Wagons were made mostly of wood with a minimum of metal parts to keep them lightweight.

The canvas top was supported by a frame of bowed wood or metal. The ends could be closed with a drawstring in bad weather.

The wooden wheels were rimmed in iron to prevent wear.

Covered wagons were pulled by horses, mules, or oxen. Given the extreme nature of the cross country journey, only the hardiest animals could be relied upon to perform. Horses were the least favored. Mules (shown above) and oxen (shown below) were sturdy alternatives, with oxen considered the more reliable, less expensive option, and almost as fast as mules.

The mid-1800s, when Eugene Chase made his overland journey, was a critical period for Native American tribes. In the one hundred years between 1800 and 1900 the population of Native American Indians in California alone was reduced by nearly 90%, from 200,000 to 15,000, mostly due to disease. Many were killed by westward settlers and government militias. This period also saw government efforts to relocate native tribes from their homelands to Indian Territory and reservations, which resulted in what were generally called the Indian Wars. Several disastrous attempts were made by the American government to remove Native Americans from east of the Mississippi River to lands west of the river. Among the tribes Eugene encountered while in the Plains were the Sioux (below left) and the Pawnee (below right).

Above: *It is estimated that in 1849 alone, approximately 90,000 gold-seekers arrived in California. By 1855 a total of 300,000 fortune hunters from around the world had arrived. The 49ers (also called the Argonauts after the ancient Greek myth that told the tale of the men who sailed with Jason on the ship "Argo" in search of the Golden Fleece) were a rough-and-tumble bunch. Their main desire was, of course, riches, and the sooner the better. For some, that reality happened. A miner could work for six months in the gold fields and walk away with the equivalent of six year's wages back home. Even ordinary prospectors averaged daily finds of gold worth ten to fifteen times the daily wage of a laborer on the East Coast.*

In addition to the best known gold strikes east of Sacramento, California there were lesser known but equally important gold fields farther north in California, primarily in and around the town of Weaverville in Trinity County. This is where Eugene Chase spent most of his time, not far from the Oregon border.

Above: *A miner pans for gold by swirling a small amount of river gravel and grit around in the pan until the heavier bits of gold sink to the bottom.* Below: *The tools needed for daily mining were few: a pick, a shovel, a pan and, for some lucky few, a "cradle" or "rocker" at bottom right. There may have been few tools, but it was back-breaking work in challenging conditions.*

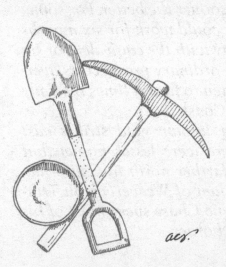

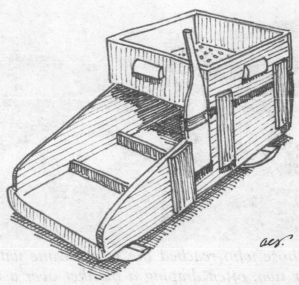

Above: *The rocker, or cradle, enabled one miner to wash twice as much gravel and soil as could be processed in the same length of time with normal panning. The apparatus was easy to transport and could be set up anywhere a source of water was available. The miner shoveled grit and gravel into the hopper, poured water over it, and rocked the cradle from side to side, sifting the material onto the apron below. As it washed along, heavier minerals, especially gold, would be stopped by the riffles in the bottom sluice and collected by hand.*

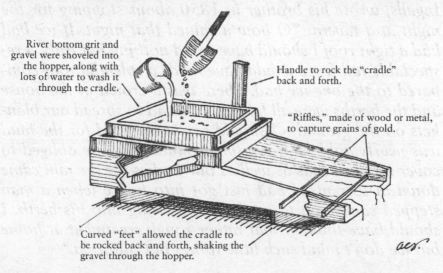

River bottom grit and gravel were shoveled into the hopper, along with lots of water to wash it through the cradle.

Handle to rock the "cradle" back and forth.

"Riffles," made of wood or metal, to capture grains of gold.

Curved "feet" allowed the cradle to be rocked back and forth, shaking the gravel through the hopper.

Most of those who reached the mines came with only a blanket or two, often draping a blanket over a ridgepole as partial protection from the elements. More enterprising miners constructed frames of logs with canvas sides and a roof. Caves and dirt dugouts also provided some protection. Toward season's end some miners built better split timber structures, as shown above. The winter of 1849-1850 was unusually wet. Some miners claimed the rain fell faster inside the cabins than outside. One goldseeker wrote that he found relief from the water leaking through the canvas roof by sleeping in a rubber cap, raincoat, and boots, with an umbrella propped over his head. Another adventurer, John Ingalls, wrote his brother in 1850 about stopping for the night at a tavern: "O how it rained that night. If we had had a tight roof I should have cared nothing but truly, a respectable rail fence would have made a splendid roof compared to the one we had. There was a crowd in the house and the berths were all taken so we had to spread our blankets on the ground – I should say in the mud for the mud was nearly ankle deep on the ground. We were obliged to cover up our heads as well as our bodies for the rain came down in torrents. I had just got into house when a man stepped square on to my head in getting into his berth. I should have thought that rather rough treatment at home but we don't mind such little things in California."

During the early years of the gold rush, there was no easy way to change mined gold into currency in order to buy goods. There were no branches of the United States Mint west of the Mississippi. Gold dust, although accepted as a means of exchange, was impractical for daily use. The first step in turning gold into money was to weigh and assay it. Assayers, working in offices like the one shown above, were trained to test the purity of gold. After weighing it,

using a scale like the one shown at right, the assayer melted the gold in a furnace and poured it into an iron mold to form a bar called an ingot. Next, the assayer cut small chips from the ingot and performed chemical analysis in order to determine its purity. Finally, the ingot was stamped with the assayer's information. Ingots could be used as currency in large transactions, such as banking or commercial use.

Afterword

In January 1969, over fifty years ago, I began teaching high school in California's Napa Valley. Hired mid-year to replace an English teacher on sabbatical, I was given her schedule: four sophomore English, and a semester elective for juniors and seniors, *Mass Media of Communication*. But of the ten candidates for the position, I was the only one with a media course on my college transcripts.

How else was I fortunate at the time? A student, Cort Sinnes, was in my media class and became a friend for life.

Now, these many decades later, Cort and I have created a new edition of a book I wrote in the the early 80s. *Along the Gold Rush Trail* was in print until 2002. Then in 2003, New Reader's Press returned the rights to me, along with the artwork, which meant I could reprint the book.

That same year, living in Lima, Peru, I recalled adolescent and adult readers who through the years had written and thanked me for Eugene's story. I thought of an article I'd saved about a man in North Carolina who learned to read as an adult. My book was the first one he ever read. Then my husband and I moved again, and the materials from New Reader's Press went into a file and were forgotten.

The desire to return to my great-great grandfather's story didn't resurface until spring 2019, when I visited a good friend in Sedona, Arizona. Carole teaches adult *English as a Second Language* (ESL) and had bought used copies of the gold rush book on the internet. One Tuesday evening I went to her ESL class and saw how positively her students responded to Eugene B. Chase's story. The students had left other countries, and they had stories to tell of survival and courageous journeys. It was these students and their dedicated teacher who inspired me to revisit the story. Yet I would not have ventured a new edition without the help of the artful, talented, soulful student from 1969 – Cort Sinnes.

In *Here to There and Back Again* I kept the story as simple as the earlier editions. Yet I relished the chance to give added voice to the story while keeping the reading level appropriate for ESL and adult literacy. In the new edition, Cort included a map of Eugene's journey West. He created a gallery of information about 1850s travel and mining for gold, which includes his own illustrations. He and I researched and found material I'd lacked in 1981. I wrote the book in a tiny German village, using an electric typewriter. I had no access to research, other than the tiny Sembach Air Force base library. How wildly different five decades later to have the internet available.

My hope is that *Here to There and Back Again* inspires readers to write stories of their lives and to leave a legacy for those who follow them, as my great-great grandfather, Eugene B. Chase, did. His letters literally changed my life; and for this I feel the deepest possible gratitude.

Gail Wilson Kenna
January 31, 2020

CPSIA information can be obtained
at www.ICGtesting.com
Printed in the USA
LVHW032125260220
648333LV00005B/5